SEBASTIAN
[Super Sleuth]
and the
Purloined Sirloin

Other books about Sebastian

Mary Blount Christian
SEBASTIAN
(Super Sleuth)
and the
Purloined Sirloin

Illustrated by LISA McCUE

MACMILLAN PUBLISHING COMPANY
New York
COLLIER MACMILLAN PUBLISHERS
London

This one's for Paula Orellana,
with special appreciation.

Macmillan Publishing Company
866 Third Avenue, New York, NY 10022
Collier Macmillan Canada, Inc.
Printed in the United States of America
10 9 8 7 6 5 4 3 2 1
The text of this book is set in 12 pt. Primer.
The illustrations are rendered in scratchboard.

Contents

1
There's Good News

Sebastian wolfed down his bowl of lightly browned, delicately seasoned ground beef. Then he wiggled excitedly while he waited for his human, John Quincy Jones, to finish his own breakfast, oatmeal with honey. Would he *ever* finish? That day, of all days, why was John so poky?

It was a big day. John and Sebastian were getting a new car—well, practically new. It was only a year old. That was quite an event in the life of an under-paid detective and his fantastic furry partner, who had no income at all. True, he, Sebastian (Super Sleuth), using all his canine know-how, solved most of John's cases for him, but he got no pay from the City Police Department. Thanks? Ha! He'd be surprised if he ever got a simple thank-you!

Because they were forced to subsist on John's pay alone, it had been four years since his human had bought a car—a well-used one, at that. Sebastian was almost as excited as John. There'd be no more breaking down right in the middle of a big car chase. No more arriving at the police station with a handcuffed criminal in a towed car. How embarrassing! Sebastian blushed through his fur, just thinking about it.

Well, now they were about to get a car more in tune with their dapper bachelor lives. A neat little sports car, a Camaro, with a sun roof and automatic door locks and rearview mirrors. Even the windshield wipers worked. Sebastian knew because he had pushed as many buttons as he could while John was squabbling with the salesman over the price. The car was just the color of a well-done barbecued roast. He twitched happily.

"Sebastian, have you got fleas again?" John asked as he ran water into his oatmeal bowl and set it in the sink. "I don't want you climbing into my new car with fleas. Maybe I should leave you home when I pick it up."

Ummmm. Ummmm. Sebastian whimpered and tried to look as hangdog as an elated canine could manage. But he was outraged, too. John had said *my* car. How could he think for one minute that the hairy hawkshaw hadn't earned his place in the front seat! Why, using his expertise and his clever disguises, Sebastian had solved case after case while John was still dallying with confusing clues. As an airline attendant, a gypsy, and even as a department-store Santa Claus—to name just a few of his famous disguises—he'd cleverly sniffed his way through puzzle after puzzle to uncover the solution and save John's job and reputation. Yes, he'd earned his place in that car, and if only he could convince some human to give him a learner's permit, he'd—

Ka whang! The mail slot cover in the front door clanged shut and broke his train of thought. *Grrrrrrrrr*, he growled, racing toward the door. Suddenly the throw rug at the entrance slid and slung him smack into the wall. *Whump!*

"Honestly, Sebastian," John complained as he followed him to the door. "You'd think you'd eventually learn about the mail carrier. He is not an intruder. Take it easy." John stooped to pick up the mail, which was scattered across the floor.

Intruder? Did John think he was stupid, or what? Sebastian knew a mail carrier from an intruder. Intruders didn't bring half-price coupons for dry dog food! Fortunately, when John was not looking, Sebastian managed to sift those from the mail and flush them down the toilet.

John reviewed the contents of the mail aloud: "A light bill, a bill from the gas company, an advertisement from that new department store." Did he think Sebastian couldn't read for himself? "And an envelope from Baxter, Rothschild, Seward,

Crump and Stumple, Attorneys-at-Law." John turned to glare at Sebastian. "We'd better not be getting sued again. You haven't been digging up any more prize rosebushes, I trust."

Sebastian glared back at John. If Mrs. Blankenbow had not planted her stupid rosebush over the exact spot where he'd buried his exceptionally tasty bone, he wouldn't have had to dig it up in the first place.

John ran his finger along the envelope, tearing it open. Sebastian eyed John anxiously, searching for a hint of expression as John read the contents of the letter. Maybe Mr. Dumbarton was tired of Sebastian's knocking over his garbage cans. Or could Ms. Mugroy be mad because he accidentally got too close to her house while they were painting it and left some of his fur on the paint? Were those grounds for a lawsuit?

But wait a minute. John's eyes were fairly dancing. He looked pleased!

"I—I don't believe it! Sebastian! Why, Sebastian, old fellow! You lovable old scamp, if only you could understand," John said as he flopped back onto the couch, laughing. "This is wonderful!"

Of course he could understand! What kind of dog did John take him for? Maybe his human just needed a little encouragement to speak. Sebastian

leaped onto the couch next to John and gave him a warm, wet kiss on the cheek.

Suddenly John jumped up and dashed into the bedroom. Sebastian followed at his heels. He watched as John rummaged through the desk drawer, tossing papers helter-skelter.

"Yes, here they are," John said. "Your pedigree papers." He scanned the papers. "Yes, yes! Your great-grandfather was Lord Cedric of Nottingham! Oh, Sebastian! Do you know what this means?"

No, he didn't know what it meant. And he was *never* going to know if John didn't quit blathering so.

John reread the letter and rechecked the pedigree papers. He whooped and threw them up in the air, catching them and whirling with a little jig. "Sir Alex Haversham, the owner of Nottingham Kennels in England, has willed his fortune to the descendants of the dogs he bred. Sebastian, you are inheriting money!"

Sebastian yelped and leaped from the floor, nipping at the air in elation. Justice at last! No more dry dog food when John's paycheck ran out before the month did. No more dirty looks from that stupid Afghan hound with the noble-sounding name down the street. From now on, he would have nothing but the best! He, Sebastian (Super Sleuth), was a hairy heir!

2
And There's Bad News

Sebastian felt giddy with excitement. Now he'd be not only clever and dashing but rich as well. He'd probably inherit a castle, or at least a tasteful but large estate somewhere in the English countryside.

"The lawyer's letter says the details will be made known soon," John said. "They have to locate the other heirs and verify your pedigree. But that's no problem. It's all right here."

John put the papers and the lawyer's letter in the drawer. "This truly calls for a celebration," John said. "A new car, and now this."

The new car! Sebastian had forgotten in the excitement of the moment. The sports car, of course. It had seemed like a wonderful car for a daring dog detective and his human. But for an heir? Wouldn't a chauffeur-driven limousine with gold-plated door trim be more appropriate?

The phone rang. John answered, flipping on the amplifier so he could change clothes while he talked.

Sebastian liked that because he could hear both sides of the conversation. It was Chief, their mean-tempered boss. At the sound of his raspy voice, Sebastian shrank against John's leg.

"Jones! I'd like you to do me a favor!" he said. It sounded more like an order than a request.

"Y–y–yessir," John said. "It's my day off, sir."

"I know that!" Chief stormed. "I wouldn't be asking if you were on duty, Jones. It's my twenty-fifth wedding anniversary tomorrow, and I want you to stop by Wright's Jewelers and pick up a sterling-silver tea service. It's already paid for. All you have to do is pick it up and bring it to me."

"Y–y–yessir," John said. "Wright's Jewelers. Pick up the tea service and bring it to you. I can do that, sir."

"And, Jones!" Chief yelled. "The set cost me a bundle. I don't want a single scratch on it. Be careful. Understand?"

"Y–y–yessir," John said. "No scratches. B–be careful. I understand."

A sudden hum on the line told Sebastian that Chief had hung up. He rolled back on his haunches and relaxed.

John sighed. "Well, we'll pick up the car, and then we'll pick up Chief's sterling-silver tea service. Any woman who would put up with that temper for

8

twenty-five years certainly deserves it!" John smiled, shrugging his shoulders slightly. "And then, my furry friend, we'll stop off at the store and pick you up the biggest, juiciest sirloin steak you ever had in your life. Nothing is too good for the descendant of Lord Cedric of Nottingham!" John laughed heartily as he grabbed a clean bedsheet, white with a morning-glory print, from the drawer.

Sebastian's ears had perked up at the mention of sirloin steak. He ran his tongue the length of his mouth, slurping up the drool he'd manufactured at the thought of that lovely meat. Pushing his chin to an appropriately aristocratic angle, he trotted out of the apartment behind John.

How thoughtful of his master to take along a sheet to cover the grimy old car seat. That noble, fuzzy bottom should not touch dirt!

John threw the sheet into the trunk, surprising Sebastian a little. Sebastian shook off his puzzlement—John probably had been confused by the exciting news—and leaped into the front passenger seat.

They drove to the car lot, where John had to sign the final papers to pick up the car. Sebastian wondered if there was a canine in the city as lucky as he was.

Hank Klutzman, the car salesman, rushed out to

them, his hand extended in greeting. He had dark black hair slicked back in a greasy pompadour and a moustache so thin it looked as if it had been drawn with a pencil. His jacket was a bright red, yellow, and green plaid. Sebastian wondered if it had been made from a horse's blanket.

While he was waiting for the salesman to bring him the papers and keys to the new car, John pulled the bedsheet from the trunk of his old car.

Sebastian wandered around the lot, looking for their car. Now that he realized he was an heir, would it seem as jaunty as he had first thought? Would it suit a dog of his new stature? What did Queen Elizabeth drive?

Then the curious canine spotted the new car near the repair garage. He trotted over and stood on his hind legs, peering through the window. Nice dashboard. It seemed appropriate for a rich dog still in touch with the common man.

Sebastian dropped to all fours. *Scratch!* Uh-oh. He'd accidentally left a long, vertical mark on the door. John would turn him into a fur wall hanging if he saw that! What could he do? Maybe he could find some compound to rub on the scratch, something to make it vanish without a trace.

He dashed into the repair garage and came to an abrupt stop when he saw the salesman, Mr. Klutzman, with a man in a greasy, paint-spattered, striped jumpsuit. It wouldn't do for them to see him. They might tell John. Sebastian slunk into a dark corner to wait.

Mr. Klutzman was counting some money as he put it into the other man's hand. "Nice job," he said. "You would never know by looking at it."

As soon as the mechanic left with his orange tow truck, Mr. Klutzman drove their car out front to John. Unfortunately, Sebastian hadn't had a chance to repair the scratch.

After John had signed the necessary papers, Mr. Klutzman gave him the keys to the new car. "Here you go," he said. "When you're ready to buy another car, you come back here now, you hear? I'll guarantee you the best deal in town."

Sebastian leaped into the car on the driver's side. Maybe he could delay John's seeing the scratch on the other door for a while.

John spread the sheet out over the front seat of the new car, rudely pushing it under Sebastian. "Stay on the sheet," he told Sebastian. "I don't want you shedding fur all over this plush brown upholstery."

Sebastian glared icily at John, then hopped onto the sheet. John had better watch it. That was *rich* fur he was talking about!

John drove to Wright's Jewelers to pick up Chief's sterling-silver tea service. Sebastian went in with

him, ignoring the store owner's scowl.

John inspected the set carefully. "I don't see any nicks or scratches," he said finally. "Please pack it and wrap it well. If anything happened to this . . ."

Sebastian knew exactly what he meant. Chief would think of something horrible to do to them, he was sure. The old super sleuth shuddered at the thought.

Sebastian trotted beside him as his human carefully carried Chief's present to the car and placed it on the back seat. John stuffed Chief's bill of sale into the glove compartment. "Get back on that sheet, Sebastian," John commanded. "And try not to shed any more than you absolutely have to."

Sebastian curled his lip. John certainly could be insensitive! He soon forgave him, though, when John pulled to a stop in front of Bagley's Butchery, which was known for its better cuts of meat.

John entered the store. Sebastian rose on his hind legs and pressed his nose against the outside of the store window. He could see John at the beef counter intently looking over several cuts of sirloin. Why make a decision? Take them all!

When John came out, Sebastian wagged the stub of his tail and eagerly touched the fragrant package with his moist, sensitive nose. *Ummmmmmmmmm.* Drool formed in the corners of his mouth.

John took a handkerchief from his pocket and

wiped Sebastian's mouth. "You'd better not drool all over the upholstery," he said. "Get in."

Grrrrrrrrr, Sebastian muttered. John was going to be a real pain about the car.

"And how would you like your celebration steak prepared tonight, milord?" John said, laughing, his good-humored self again.

Sebastian closed his eyes, imagining. Barbecued? Raw? How about medium rare, smothered in mush-

room gravy? *Ummmmmmmmm.*

"We'll just stop off a minute at Maude's and show her the new wheels," John said. "Then we'll get Chief's tea service to him before something happens to it and we get blamed."

Oh, no, Sebastian thought. Why did John have to stop at Maude's? The old hairy hawkshaw, noble heir to a fortune, could understand John's wanting to drop off Chief's tea service before it got ruined. But why complicate things by stopping at Maude's? John was getting too serious about Maude Culpepper, in Sebastian's opinion. Ever since John's mother had introduced him to Maude, he'd been dating her. They spent entirely too much time together. Next thing you knew they would be making plans for marriage. Perish the thought!

He, Sebastian (Super Sleuth), would never give up his bachelor life. And if John were smart, neither would he. Besides, Maude had Lady Sharon, and, as far as Sebastian was concerned, there was room for only one Old English sheepdog in the family.

Sebastian broke into a panting grin at the thought of Lady Sharon's reaction to his becoming a rich dog. He planned to carry *his* royal title with more dignity and grace than she did *her* title (which was only honorary, anyway)!

John pulled up in front of Maude's town house. "Come on, boy. Let's go surprise Maude." When

Sebastian had gotten out, John locked the doors.

Sebastian glanced back longingly at his sirloin. He hated to leave it in the car. But he certainly didn't want to carry it into the house and let Lady Sharon get a whiff of it!

He trotted to the front door with John. Maude swung open the door and greeted John. Lady Sharon trotted up and touched Sebastian's nose with hers.

He got a whiff of her *Ode de Doggie* perfume and sneezed. *Ah-hoooey!* What did she see in that smelly stuff anyway? It seemed downright unnatural for a dog to smell like that!

When they were inside, John quickly told Maude about Sebastian's inheritance. Sebastian blushed as Maude reached down to pat his head in con-gratulations. He backed away, sure that red showed right through his fur. As soon as people knew you were rich, they were all over you!

"And," John said, waving his car keys in front of Maude, "I got it!"

Maude looked out the window. "Wonderful, but why didn't you drive it over?"

"I did!" John said. "It's right there in front of— Oh, no!"

Sebastian spun around to look toward the street. The car was gone! Some dastardly thief had stolen it! Somebody had purloined his sirloin!

3
A Hot Clue

Sebastian dashed to the street and sniffed. He ran around in circles, barking in frustration. How mean could a thief get? How could he take a dog's first sirloin in months?

John's face was pale. "My new car! And—oh, no! —Chief's sterling-silver tea service!" He moaned as he raced back to Maude's house to phone in the report to the police. "Chief will be furious! He'll probably fire me!"

"I'll get my station wagon!" Maude called. "Maybe we can spot it!"

It was not only distressing; it was downright embarrassing. The greatest dog detective in the world had had a juicy, two-inch-thick steak—and a car with a sterling-silver tea service—stolen right from under his sensitive nose. Chief would never let him and his human live that down! Maybe Chief would not let him and his human live, period!

John called in the report. Then Maude got out her

station wagon, and she, John, Sebastian, and Lady Sharon rode up and down the streets, trying to find the car.

When John finally admitted there was no sign of it, Maude drove them to the police station. They went straight to the auto-theft division.

"I called in the theft at exactly one P.M.," John told Officer Jim Kallon. "That couldn't have been more than three minutes after the car was stolen. It's now four P.M. And I read you the license number and even the motor-vehicle serial number right off the sales contract. Why hasn't a patrol officer spotted the car? Surely the thief will abandon it when he's finished joyriding. And he'd just leave Chief's tea service, wouldn't he?"

Officer Kallon grabbed his own neck and made a choking sign. "You lost Chief's tea service? I'd hate to be in your shoes, Jones! Listen, once in a while kids break into a car and hot-wire it and drive it until it runs out of gas," Officer Kallon said. "But your car is pretty new. I bet it's the victim of a chop shop. That tea service is probably in a pawn shop, and your car's probably a pile of parts by now."

"A pawn shop! Parts!" John roared. "My car, a pile of parts? Oh, boy, I don't know which is worse!"

What about his sirloin? Sebastian wondered. Would those heartless beasts turn it into *chopped* beef? Or, perish the thought, *ground* beef? *Grrrrrrrrr.*

"But why wouldn't they keep the car just like it is?" John protested. "Surely they wouldn't chop up a practically new car."

"Parts of a car sell individually for more money than the car as a whole, John," Officer Kallon said. "You ever had anything repaired? You know how expensive it is to replace car parts? Besides, parts aren't as easy to trace as a whole car."

John shook his head sadly. "How could anybody cut up that beautiful little car?"

Or his sirloin? Sebastian wondered, his chin between his paws.

The dispatcher yelled over the counter, "Hey, Kallon. We got an abandoned car report."

"Where?" John asked. "Maybe it's mine. I'll go check it out."

"Where Frontage Road and Farm Road Twelve cross, but—"

"Thanks!" John said without waiting for the rest of the news. He dashed out the precinct door. Maude, Lady Sharon, and Sebastian ran to catch up.

They drove along Frontage Road, but they couldn't even reach the point where it crossed Farm Road Twelve. A fire engine was blocking the way, and the firefighters were spraying water on something.

Sebastian followed John through the tangle of water hoses to see what was on fire.

What Sebastian saw made his heart sink to his toes. There, at the side of the road, was the burned-out frame of a car, the same size as their car. Its doors were missing. Its engine was gone. It had no tires or wheels. Even the seats were gone. There was little left to this car but the skeleton. And the thief must have taken Chief's tea service, too. Otherwise, the fire would have melted it, and there would still be traces of the shiny metal around.

"*Ohhhhh.*" John moaned. "I hope that isn't *my* beautiful little car."

One of the firefighters came over to John. "Not much left of this baby," he said. "We get a couple of calls a day about these smoldering shells left on the streets. Oh, sometimes the culprit's a car owner who has a real lemon and can't get rid of it any other way. He figures he'll get the insurance money and get the car off his back.

"It was especially bad during that gas shortage. The old gas-guzzlers were going up in smoke all over town. But these professional thieves, they chop 'em up, take everything usable, then set the remains afire. They figure they can destroy the evidence that way."

When the metal had cooled, Sebastian sniffed around the blackened frame. On the back floor was something that resembled an old shoe heel. It was dark and brittle. He stuck his nose to it. *Ah-hoooey!*

Was that tough, still smoldering chunk of un-identified matter all that was left of his beautiful, tender, succulent sirloin steak? *Grrrrrrrrr!* Nobody did that to sirloin—especially *his* sirloin—and got away with it. And what about Chief's tea service? And his poor human's first car in years? Somebody was going to pay for this. He, Sebastian (Super Sleuth)—and ruggedly handsome heir to a fortune —promised himself he would not rest until he had the dastardly thief behind bars.

4
On the Trail

Sebastian waded through the puddles of water left by the firefighters. His tummy rumbled, reminding him of the steak he was not going to have that night and making him even more determined to find the thief. Why hadn't the thief removed the steak before setting fire to the car? Surely he would have wanted the succulent, tasty sirloin for himself. After all, he *had* removed the silver tea service.

The arson-division officers combed through the remains of the car, looking for any clues. "See this heavier burn in the trunk," one of the men said, "and here across the floor. It's in a pattern indicating that flammable liquid was used. This fire was deliberately set, all right."

John stood there, his hands in his pockets, nervously jingling the keys that were now useless. "Well, I'll report the theft to the insurance company right now. Then I have to go face Chief with the news about his silver tea service. Then I'm going to solve this case, if it's the last thing I ever do," he said angrily.

And what about the old hairy hawkshaw! He had a stake—or was that *steak?*—in the crime, too. Sebastian wondered if they had a sirloin-theft division. Never mind. He'd join John in the auto-theft division and find the sadistic sirloin thief. The thief would pay! He stopped to lap water that was puddled near the curb.

What was that, floating in the water? Sebastian slapped his big paw over the object and worked it out of the puddle before it could be swept into the drain. A matchbook cover—empty. It said:

JOE'S AUTO SUPPLIES.

BEST DEALS IN TOWN

FOR BUYERS AND SELLERS.

Auto supplies? Parts? Buyers and sellers? Hadn't Officer Kallon said thieves sold the cars in parts? Maybe Joe's Auto Supplies could offer the best deals in town because Joe hadn't paid anything for the parts—because he had stolen them! The clever canine hawkshaw figured this could be a valuable lead to the dastardly meat maimers. He barked to get John's attention.

"Hush, Sebastian," John said crossly. "I'm in no mood to put up with your shenanigans right now."

Maude was standing at the edge of the crowd that had gathered, holding back Lady Sharon. "Come, Sebastian!" she called. "Come here, boy. Stay with us!"

Sebastian eyed her sharply. Didn't she know it was against the law to interfere with the investigation of a crime? He closed his teeth around the valuable clue, then trotted over to the car frame. He dropped the matchbook cover near the car. It was visible enough for John or one of the other detectives to find it. But it was hidden just enough so they wouldn't wonder how they had missed it in the first place.

John walked slowly around the car skeleton, shaking his head, muttering about his stolen car and Chief's sterling-silver tea service. Sebastian sat by the matchbook cover, his stub of a tail wagging eagerly, his lips parted in a panting grin, waiting for John to spot it. But John overlooked the clue!

Sebastian grabbed it once more and raced around to the other side of the car. He dropped it on the road near the car.

John walked over. "Here, what's this?" he asked, much to Sebastian's relief. "Joe's Auto Supplies, is it? Well, we'll just see about that. Hmmm."

Sebastian leaped into the station wagon next to Lady Sharon. Maude drove them to the police station. She and Lady Sharon waited in the car while the two detectives went in.

First John called his insurance agent, who assured him the company would replace the car if it wasn't found, or if it turned out to be the smoldering skeleton. The man told John that the insurance company would not replace the silver tea service, however. Sebastian figured that meant his sirloin steak wouldn't be replaced by the insurance company, either. Finally, the agent told John that they would lend him a car until his new car had been found or replaced.

That settled, John went to see Chief. Chief's face got darker and darker as John told him what had happened. "You—you lost my sterling-silver tea service? Why, you numbskull! You miserable . . ." Chief wagged a fat finger under John's nose. "The only reason I'm not going to fire you is that I want to make sure you earn the money to replace that tea service!"

John flushed. "You'll have your silver tea service. I guarantee it, Chief! I feel just awful about this. Sebastian is coming into an inheritance, and as soon as he gets it—"

"I have no intention of making the missus wait for her anniversary present!" Chief said. "I won't have her thinking I forgot our anniversary and just came up with a silly excuse for not having a present. You had better get it—or another one just like it—before our celebration tomorrow." Chief's face was about the color of a raw steak.

Sebastian curled his lip. What was Chief getting so excited about? There was no comparison between a metal tea service and a juicy, tender steak! His tummy rumbled.

"I want to be temporarily transferred to the auto-theft division," John said. "I feel sure that if we find *our* thief we'll find the ring that's been operating around the city."

How could John say *if* we find the thief? *When* was the correct word. Sebastian had every intention of finding him. He was not going to get away with stealing a steak from the hairy heir.

"I already have a clue that I want to follow up on," John said. "Joe's Auto Supplies sounds like a good place to start looking."

Sebastian rose on his hind legs and put two paws on Chief's desk. He spotted a bowl of chili, buttered crackers, and a cup of instant cocoa. He sniffed, absorbing the inviting aroma.

"Down!" Chief shouted at Sebastian. To John he mumbled, "Transfer to school patrol if it will get me my stolen silver tea service and get that four-legged garbage can out of my office!"

How could the Chief begrudge him a little taste of chili when Sebastian had lost his succulent sirloin? He couldn't be that heartless. *Slurp!* He swallowed Chief's chili in one easy gulp. *Snap! Snap!* He snatched the crackers. The cocoa he'd leave for Chief. After all, *he* was not heartless.

Chief flew into a tirade about his lost bowl of chili. But Sebastian trotted out of Chief's office without even glancing back.

John stopped off to tell Lt. Helen Cranston of the auto-theft division that he would be working with them for a while. She shared what little information they already had.

"We know they're extremely organized and professional," she said. "They can steal, strip, and abandon a car in a matter of hours. They're everywhere, roaming the city, looking for potential victims."

"I know," John muttered. "I know."

"We think they have other methods of getting rid of whole cars, too. But so far we haven't stopped one suspicious vehicle without proper papers," she said.

"Well, I'm going to follow up on this Joe's Auto Supplies," John said. "But I don't want to scare anyone into hiding. I'll go undercover."

Ah-ha, Sebastian thought. At last John was

adopting his own clever method of detection. Together they would bring the meat thief to justice.

Of course, he, Sebastian (Super Sleuth), would have to do the bulk of the work—as usual.

5
On the Road Again

Maude drove John and Sebastian to Rent-a-Rattletrap, where the insurance man sent them for their substitute car. The car they got looked worse than the old car they'd traded in, but at least it had wheels.

And now they wouldn't have to depend on Maude to get around. Sebastian had had enough of Lady Sharon and her kissy-kissy ways. True, he couldn't blame her for falling victim to his natural charm. But her behavior *was* distracting.

Sebastian and John crawled into the ten-year-old car with crumpled fenders and a wired-on front bumper and drove home. It was late, and Joe's Auto Supplies was already closed for the day.

They found Maude and Lady Sharon waiting on their doorstep with a casserole for supper. Maude said she was afraid John would be too upset to cook anything. She was right. He was also too upset to eat and scraped the food from his plate into the garbage.

Sebastian was too upset *not* to eat and finished his own un-sirloin supper, then retrieved John's from the garbage pail. *Burp!*

He tried to think of more pleasant things, such as his English manor in the countryside with butlers in morning coats bringing his tea biscuits and tenderloins onto the terrace. He fell asleep, dreaming of meeting the Queen. Did a canine curtsy or merely wag his tail?

The next morning—before they'd even had a proper three-course breakfast—they drove to Joe's Auto Supplies. It was a rusted metal building surrounded by a high wire fence. Inside the fence were fenders, radiators, doors, and bumpers from cars of every imaginable style and year.

John and Sebastian went inside the building. Sebastian noticed a vending machine with peanut-butter crackers, corn chips, and sandwiches. Ah, ham and cheese. Sebastian pushed the buttons, hoping some jammed quarter would fall into place and yield him a goody. Nothing happened. He stuck his nose to the trough and inhaled deeply. No goody tumbled to greet him. He sighed his disappointment and joined John.

Behind the counter a man with one eyebrow that

stretched across both eyes and tattoos on both arms said he was Joe. "Whatcha lookin' for?" he asked. "If it ain't here now, it can be by four o'clock."

Sebastian glared at the man. He just bet it could! That guy probably had thieves roaming the city streets, ready to fill orders! Had someone ordered a fender, or a door maybe, of a Camaro the color of well-done barbecued roast? Sebastian's tummy rumbled hungrily at the thought.

"I need a right-front quarter panel for a 1985 Camaro," John said. "And I sure hate to pay dealer prices."

Joe scowled. "An '85?" He tapped the keys on the gray computer on the counter. "Nothing on the lot right now. But I can have it here by four, just like the sign says."

"That's amazing!" John said. "How do you know you can get exactly what I want? And so soon?"

Joe's eyebrow formed into the deep vee of a scowl. "That's my business secret," he said. "I don't tell no business secrets. It might leak out to the competition."

"Of course," John said. "I understand. I'll be back this afternoon."

With a warrant for his arrest! Sebastian hoped. He lifted his nose into the air and sniffed. No meat there.

They left. That is, they left the building. But they couldn't get the rented wreck started. John opened the hood. Sebastian rose on his hind legs, leaned against the fender, and peered inside. There sure were a lot of gadgets in there. Which one could keep the car from starting?

John wiggled the wires. He took off his shoe and hammered on anything he could reach. Sebastian knew John had no idea what he was doing. Unfortunately, his own knowledge of auto mechanics was limited, too. At least when he came into his inheritance he could let the chauffeur worry about such things.

Brummmmm, brummmmm. A 1968 Camaro with chrome dual exhaust pipes and a shiny blue paint job pulled up next to them. A tall, thin teenager with a shock of dark hair over his forehead and freckles across his nose jumped out.

"Hi," the boy said, leaning both hands on the edge of the hood. "Got a problem with your car, mister? Great dog!"

Sebastian's mouth parted in a panting grin. There was a smart kid. Good taste.

"This isn't my car," John said defensively. "It's a rental. I have—had—an '85 Camaro."

"Stolen, huh?" the boy asked. "That's what happened to my first one. I don't let this one out of

my sight, believe me! Boy, I get furious when I think of someone stealing a car. Sometimes I think I'd like to become a cop and hunt them all down."

He wiggled the battery cable. "There's your trouble. Contact is bad. See how corroded the cable attachments are? Just a second." He got a bottle— he said it was vinegar—a wrench, and a stiff brush from the trunk of his car. "I keep stuff handy, just in case," he said. He worked a minute, then said, "Now try to start the car."

John got in and turned on the ignition.

"Pump the gas pedal," the boy said.

The motor turned over. Sebastian leaped with joy and yipped happily. John left the motor running and got out and thanked the boy for his help.

"That's a great-looking car you have, a real classic," John said. "This is your second one, you say? Oh, by the way, I'm John Quincy Jones. What did you say your name was?"

"Thanks, Mr. Jones. Dave Blum's the name. After my first one was stolen, I bought this one for two hundred and fifty dollars. It was a piece of junk. But I rebuilt it in school, in auto-mechanics class," Dave Blum said. "It won second place in district school competition."

"That's not much to pay for a car," John said. "Where did you find such a bargain?"

"At the police auction," Dave said. "You can get some pretty good deals there if you don't mind bidding against the people who redo and sell cars for a living."

The police auction! Of course! Why had he needed a teenage boy to remind him about it? That was a natural place to look. The thief could well be a professional car rebuilder who had to buy *some* of the things he needed.

6
Going, Going, Gone!

Before going to the police auction, John called the auto-theft division. Sebastian scratched his ear impatiently while John seemed to get more and more excited. How frustrating to hear only one side of a conversation!

"Uh-huh. Uh-huh. . . . Really? The plates with the serial number were missing from the dashboard and under the hood? You mean the serial number I read off the sales contract appears all over the car?" John asked. "I thought it was put only on the dashboard. . . . Oh, it's hidden in other places! But why would the thief remove the serial number? Why would he care if anyone knew to whom a burned, abandoned car was registered?"

If the burned frame didn't have a single serial number on it, it would be hard to know if it was their car. Though there *had* been that pathetically tough piece of sirloin in the back, which of course John hadn't noticed.

But John was right. It was curious that the thief would bother to remove the serial number, unless he needed it for something else. But what?

"Fingerprints! From a burned-out frame? . . . You can? That's fantastic!"

Sebastian wagged the stub of his tail. Fingerprints. Modern technology was wonderful! He'd seen on some television cop show that they could lift fingerprints from burned, scorched metal, but he'd thought it was only a figment of the writer's imagination.

"No match with fingerprints on file. Well, maybe if we get a lead we'll find the guy who torched the car. Then we'll have some fingerprints for comparison. . . . The heel of a shoe? Will that help?"

A shoe heel? Then it was a toughened piece of leather he'd found and not the cremated remains of a succulent, four-inch sirloin steak! That meant there was still a chance that his sirloin—the car, too, of course—was still around. Oh, joy! Sebastian licked the drool that formed on his fuzzy lips.

John hung up, and they drove to the police compound. Wherever Sebastian looked there were cars parked in neat little rows. People wandered up and down the rows.

John walked around, looking. But apparently he didn't see anything suspicious, either.

"Hi, Mr. Jones!" somebody said. "You finding everything you need?"

It was Dave, the boy they had met at Joe's Auto Supplies.

"Hello again," John greeted him. "I wasn't looking for anything in particular. Just, er, scouting around."

"Yeah, it's fun," Dave said, reaching down to tweek Sebastian's ears. "All the abandoned cars get auctioned off for terrific prices. Not that you don't have to tow 'em away. They sure aren't in running condition. And you wouldn't be caught dead driving them, even if you could. They all look like fugitives from Rent-a-Rattletrap."

Sebastian blushed, remembering that was where they had secured their own car replacement, which was far below the standard for a royal heir. Would Lord Sebastian do his detective work in a car from Rent-a-Rattletrap? No way!

"These auctions last until around noon, or until the cars are all sold—whether to private buyers, mechanics, or junk dealers. But you need to get here early if you want a really good one. The newer models go pretty fast."

"Why would anybody abandon a late model?"

John asked, voicing Sebastian's own thought.

Dave shrugged. "Oh, you know. They get totaled from a wreck, and maybe they aren't covered by insurance. So they're brought to the compound. And pretty soon the towing and storing charges mount up to more than the wrecked car is worth. Some owners just leave them. They figure it's cheaper to abandon them than pay them out. I think the police compound has to keep the cars in storage only ninety days before impounding them for auction."

"I don't understand," John said. "If these cars are in such awful shape, why would somebody want to buy them?"

Dave chucked Sebastian under the chin, causing Sebastian's back foot to thump rhythmically. "By the time some of these mechanics get through with them, you'd think they had never been damaged at all. Shoot, if I hadn't seen their registration papers myself, I'd swear they weren't the same cars!"

Sebastian nuzzled Dave's hand appreciatively. He seemed like an all-right kind of guy. And he had been most helpful to the dynamic dog and his human.

He had not only helped them get that wreck of a rental car on the road again (thereby avoiding the embarrassment of calling for a tow truck and probably another tirade from Chief), but Dave had also provided them with a place to look for clues.

That abandoned car frame really bothered Sebastian. If the car had been burned to collect insurance, the owners would *want* it traced back to them so they could get the money. The last thing they would do was remove the number.

But if it was a thief who had taken all the parts and burned the car, why would he want to take the number, which, unlike parts, was traceable?

Nothing seemed to fit. If only he could find his sirloin, everything would fall into place. His stomach growled. If only he could find his sirloin, period!

Sebastian strolled up and down the rows, sniffing the tires, peering inside. Several of the cars were late models, no more than a year or two old. The newest car there was a totaled 1984 Corvette with a crumpled front end and no windows.

Sebastian pulled back suddenly when he saw a man in a greasy, paint-spattered jumpsuit. It was the same man who had been at the car lot the day before, when they had picked up their car. He was working for Klutzman, the car dealer. Sebastian had overheard Klutzman telling him, "You would never know by looking." Know what? That the car had been a wreck? Or that it had been stolen? That man would bear watching.

A man wearing a white straw hat and carrying a wooden gavel climbed onto a small platform. "Bid on car one," he said. "Who'll start the bidding?"

The man in the greasy, paint-spattered, striped jumpsuit shouted, "Twenty-five dollars!"

"Twentyfivetwentyfivewho'llmakeitfiftyfiftyfifty who'llmakeitonehundredonehundred," the man shouted. He repeated the words as if they were all one word.

The car they were bidding on was the Corvette. Sebastian doubted that anyone could ever fix it, and it looked as if it didn't even have enough whole parts to sell at Joe's Auto Supplies. Still, the man in the greasy, paint-spattered, striped jumpsuit kept bidding. The bidding shut off at two hundred and fifty dollars. That would be a wonderful price for a repairable Corvette. But for that one? He was certainly not getting a bargain.

Sebastian edged closer to the man, who went up to give the auctioneer a check for the car and get the registration papers. He sniffed at the man's footprints. That was odd. One shoe heel made a wavy line pattern; the other made little circles.

John was so absorbed in watching the bidding that he ignored Sebastian's tugging at his coat sleeve. Well, if he couldn't get his human to check into the clues at hand, he would have to do it himself. Sebastian leaped into the Corvette. What was so appealing about that wrecked car? he wondered. If the man was stealing nice cars, why did he need that hunk of junk?

Suddenly something jolted the car. There was a grinding sound, and the car tilted. The man was hooking it to his tow truck! Sebastian cringed in the seat. *Thump!* A striped jumpsuit and a mechanic's hat landed on top of him. Then the car lurched forward.

Sebastian peeked from beneath the jumpsuit. He was being taken out of the police compound in a wrecked Corvette by his prime suspect!

7

In the Nick of Crime

Sebastian got up and looked out the back window, hoping John would see him and follow. He yelped to get his human's attention.

"Wait!" John shouted. "My dog!" But the man kept towing.

John dashed toward the rental car and jumped inside. Sebastian's heart quickened. Would John be able to keep up in that old rattletrap? Oh, no! John was getting out and opening the hood. The car wouldn't start again! He could see Dave running over to John's car. Maybe Dave could get it started!

There was nothing Sebastian could do but ride along with the man. He would make his escape when he could—if he could.

He dared not let the man catch him in the car. What could he do? His keen mind snapped to attention. He would disguise himself! He would put on the mechanic's clothes, then steal away un-

noticed once the man had reached his destination.

Quickly Sebastian slipped into the mechanic's striped jumpsuit. He wiggled under the cap, hiding as much of his handsome profile as he could beneath the bill.

The car rumbled on. Sebastian crawled to the front of the car and into the shadows beneath the crumpled dashboard. At last the car stopped. Sebastian stayed hidden until the count of ten, then dared to peek over the edge of the window. They were inside a big metal building. Everywhere he looked there were cars—nice-looking cars and wrecks like the one just towed in.

There were more men—four altogether—in greasy, paint-spattered, striped jumpsuits, all busy working on the cars. Silently Sebastian crept out of the car and crouched among some barrels, waiting for his chance to escape. He sniffed, sensing a variety of odors—grease, paint, rust, and meat. Meat? Sirloin meat?

He rose on his hind legs, leaned against the barrel, and looked in. It was a trash barrel. Inside was a big piece of butcher paper. Sebastian struggled to read the pricing tape, which was torn. It said "ley's Bu." Could that be a fragment of Bagley's Butchery? Had that piece of delicious-smelling paper held his very own sirloin steak?

His very own tender, juicy, six-inch sirloin had been in there. And now it was gone! That man had *eaten* his sirloin!

A low rumble grew in his throat. Nobody was going to eat his steak and get away with it! *Grrrrrrrrrr.*

He nosed around in the trash some more. There was a sales slip from Wright's Jewelers for one silver tea service. And there were some little metal plates with numbers on them, too. One of the numbers looked familiar. It was the serial number for *their* car! (Being the thorough detective he was, he'd memorized the number when John had called in the report.) Was that all that was left of their little sports car—its serial number?

"Hey, Harry! Quit hanging around the trash barrel and get to work!" the man who had brought him there yelled. "We got to get these numbers done and get these cars out of here."

Sebastian's head snapped up. Had he said, "Hey, hairy?" Yes, the man was calling him. He snatched a wrench between his teeth and trotted over to the man.

"Remove the serial number off that Corvette I just brought in," the man said. "And hurry up. We ought to have a match pretty soon."

Sebastian mumbled under his breath. He knew that was the man who had eaten his sirloin. It had to be. The miserable meat maimer! But what did he mean,"get the serial number off"? What did he mean by "have a match"? The man talked in riddles.

Sebastian dog-trotted toward the Corvette as the man had directed (no need to arouse his suspicion by disobeying), but a car in the shadows caught his attention. It was a Camaro—a brown one, the color of a well-done barbecued roast beef. Could it be? Sebastian rose on his hind legs and looked through the window at the serial number on the driver's side of the dashboard. No, that number was different.

48

Hmmmmm. Their serial number was in the trash barrel not five feet away. And this dashboard had a different number. But there was also a hairline scratch on the dashboard. Had a tool made that scratch? No doubt. The man probably had taken off their number and thrown it away. But where had he gotten the new number? Of course! He'd gotten it from an old car that he'd bought legally! But how could Sebastian be sure?

Then he remembered. He dashed around to the other side of the car. Sure enough, there was a scratch, vertical and about a claw wide. He peeked inside. There on the seat was a white sheet with a morning-glory print. It *was* their own car! That man had stolen their car. It hadn't been chopped up at all! If only his wonderful sirloin had been so lucky!

The same car with a different serial number. That's what the man had meant! He'd meant remove the serial-number plates from the Corvette. He had meant he was going to steal a matching car in good shape and switch the numbers. That was how the cars were always properly registered. The man bought a late-model, wrecked car at the auction to get correct and legal papers on it. Then he stole a similar car in excellent condition and switched the plates. Clever—but not as clever as the cagey canine, Sebastian (Super Sleuth)!

"Cops!" one of the men yelled, holding his hands high in the air. There was a commotion as the other mechanics scrambled around, running into one another before gathering in a circle with their hands above their heads.

Sebastian peered from behind the car to see a shiny blue 1968 Camaro pull up outside. There was a patrol car right behind it. John got out with Dave. Two patrolmen followed him in.

"For heaven's sake, put your hands down," John said. "I didn't mean to startle you fellows. Which one of you towed the Corvette from the police compound?" John asked the group of mechanics, who didn't seem to know whether to put their hands in the air or in their pockets.

But the man who had done the towing was trying to slip out through a back window. Sebastian made a mad dash to the window and snapped at the seat of his pants, hauling him back in. No sirloin thief was going to get away!

Sebastian nudged the man toward the group of mechanics, who quickly pointed him out in answer to John's question. Meanwhile Sebastian wriggled out of his disguise.

"Didn't you hear me yelling at you at the compound?" John asked.

"I . . . I . . ." the man said. He glanced around nervously, looking confused.

"My dog was in your car," John said. "I'm really sorry about that. I'm sure he didn't do any damage. But where is he?"

"Dog?" the man said. "A dog? You're here about a dog that stowed away in my car?" He sniggered nervously. The other mechanics laughed, too.

Sebastian dashed out from his hiding place to greet John. If only he could make him understand what was going on. There they were, right in the middle of the car-theft ring with two patrolmen to back them up, and John didn't know he had the thieves.

He leaped up at John, yelping excitedly.

"There you are, you naughty fellow," John scolded. "Shame on you! Do you know what trouble you caused, stowing away like that? I made Dave here chase after you, a tad above the speed limit. And that made Patrolman Smith chase after us and—"

Sebastian tugged at John's arm, pulling him toward their car.

"My, my, but you certainly do excellent work," John said. "Look at these cars. Why, you can't tell they'd ever been wrecked."

He ran his hand across the hood of the brown Camaro. "This one particularly catches my eye. It reminds me of my own new car." John leaned over, his eyebrow arched suspiciously, and read the serial number on the dashboard. He sighed, obviously satisfied that it was not his car.

Sebastian leaped through the open window and tugged at the bedsheet that still lay on the front seat. He whined, begging John to take special notice.

"I'm sorry!" John said. "Here, now, Sebastian. Mind your manners. Isn't it enough that you—" He frowned. "Wait a minute. I'd know those purple morning glories anywhere! That's my bedsheet on the front seat! How—"

Sebastian dashed over to the trash barrel and, with a mighty leap, knocked it over. The plates with the serial number clattered to the concrete floor.

John whirled around. "Gentlemen, I believe *now* you can put your hands in the air. Patrolman Smith, I think you'd better call for the paddy wagon. We're going to need a very large conveyance for these thieves. And, while you're calling in, please inform Lt. Cranston that I have her car-theft ring here."

Sebastian slumped to a sitting position, exhausted. Sometimes it was so hard to make humans understand what was going on. Now, if he could just get John to admit that he, Sebastian (Super Sleuth), had had something to do with the solution!

8
Dashed Dreams

Back at the Chief's office, Sebastian curled his lip and rumbled a protest. John was still taking all the credit. Humans! At least John took all the blame for losing Chief's silver tea service. Fair was fair.

What surprised the old hawkshaw, though, was Chief's attitude toward the lost tea service. He even said John didn't have to replace it. He probably wanted John in his debt, the cagey canine figured.

Sebastian was relieved when John insisted on buying Chief a new service. He surely didn't want to owe Chief, either. And he, Sebastian (Super Sleuth), didn't mind John's using a smidgen of the inheritance to buy Chief a silver tea service. What was money among friends?

He did look forward to more news about his inheritance—and to a leisurely drive in their new car, which they had gotten back. But before leaving

Chief's office they had to piece together all the information they had gathered.

It seemed the thief had seen John picking up the car from Klutzman and, since he had purchased a similar wreck recently, had decided to follow them and steal it the first chance he got.

Joe of Joe's Auto Supplies was not involved. The parts Joe got from the thief, who insisted his name was John Doe, came from Doe's legally purchased clunkers. Joe said the reason he had guaranteed that he could get any part a customer needed by afternoon was that he was in a computer hookup with other junkyards, not because he got special orders from the thief.

Klutzman wasn't involved, either, although he had bought some of the "refurbished" cars from John Doe without knowing that they were really stolen cars.

Naturally John Doe's fingerprints matched those that had been lifted from the burned-out car frame. All in all, the case against him was a good one.

"If Sebastian hadn't accidentally been towed away in that Corvette," John said, "I'd have had no reason at all to suspect that man."

Accidentally? John just didn't give the old hawk-shaw any credit at all, did he? Sebastian blushed slightly. Well, it may have been a *little* accidental.

"When he got to the chop shop, he was probably terrified at being in a strange place. He must have smelled the familiar bedsheet and been reminded of home. Of course he'd go for the familiar. I saw that he was tugging at the bedsheet, which I recognized as my own."

Oh, how John twisted things to avoid praising the cagey canine for his daring detective work. Well, at least John had told Chief about the important part Dave Blum had played in solving the case. The Chief decided to give Dave a citation for bravery. And since Dave had the good taste to think that Sebastian was a great dog, Sebastian felt *almost* as if he'd been commended himself. Almost. Thank goodness he'd have his tidy inheritance to soothe his hurt feelings!

John drove them home in the new car. He put a big chain and padlock around its axle and hooked it to a big oak tree. Nobody was going to steal it again!

John was reheating some stew for supper when the doorbell rang. "I'm Samuel Freeman of Baxter, Rothschild, Seward, Crump and Stumple, Attorneys-at-Law," the young man said.

"Freeman?" John said. You aren't Baxter, Rothschild, Seward, Crump, or Stumple?"

"I'm not a partner yet," Mr. Freeman said. "I'm

here in regard to the inheritance mentioned in the letter."

"Oh, yes!" John said. "Do come in! How exciting! My own Sebastian, an heir."

Sebastian wiggled excitedly and gave the man's hand a warm nuzzle.

When they were all seated, Mr. Freeman pulled a letter from his briefcase. "As you were told in your copy of the letter, the late Sir Alex Haversham, the owner of Nottingham Kennels in Devonshire, England, had no human heirs. He therefore bequeathed his holdings to the descendants of the dogs he had bred."

Sebastian licked his chops. Oh, boy! Vast riches! Pheasant under glass! Chicken cordon bleu. Rock cornish hen glazed in orange sauce!

Mr. Freeman cleared his throat nervously. "Uh, of course, when you consider that each litter may average six puppies, and they grow up to have litter after litter of six puppies, and—"

John frowned. "Yes, I know all about that. What exactly are you getting at?"

The young lawyer shrugged. "I'm afraid that once we divided his holdings among all those generations of puppies, there wasn't all that much apiece." He shoved the check toward John.

John stared openmouthed at the check. "Five

hundred and one dollars and forty-nine cents? That's it?"

Mr. Freeman shrugged. "Sorry. I hope you didn't get your hopes up too much."

Sebastian felt like a kicked puppy. His dreams of an estate, of limitless supplies of flaming meals on sterling trays, gone in a poof. At least he had five hundred and one dollars and forty-nine cents. That should buy a lot of sirloin!

When Mr. Freeman had left, John sighed. "Oh, well, Sebastian, easy come, easy go. Tell you what. We'll go down to Wright's Jewelers and get that five-hundred-dollar sterling-silver tea service."

Sebastian's lips turned under at the thought of

losing all his lovely sirloins. But it would be worth the sacrifice to get Chief off their backs.

"That will leave exactly a dollar forty-nine, which will get you a double burger and a small order of french fries at the corner quick-stop. What do you say we blow the whole inheritance all at once? And let's invite that nice boy Dave to go with us. He was a great help, don't you think? With a little encouragement, he might even think about becoming one of us when he graduates."

A dog? Why would Dave— Oh, a detective! Of course, Sebastian thought. Dave would be a great detective—not as great as he, Sebastian (Super Sleuth), but certainly as good as John. And, besides, Dave had terrific taste in dogs, and he knew just where to scratch the ears. Ummmm.

Sebastian perked up. A double burger? With french fries? He sighed. No English manor. No butlers. No tea biscuits. Ah, well. No IRS breathing down his neck over inheritance taxes. And no fortune hunters yipping at his feet, either. If he was especially careful not to shed fur on their new car interior, maybe John would throw in a slice of apple pie for dessert.

And there would always be yet another criminal out there with whom to match wits. Sebastian licked his chops. Life wasn't so bad, after all!